characters created by lauren child

I completely KNOW about guinea pigs

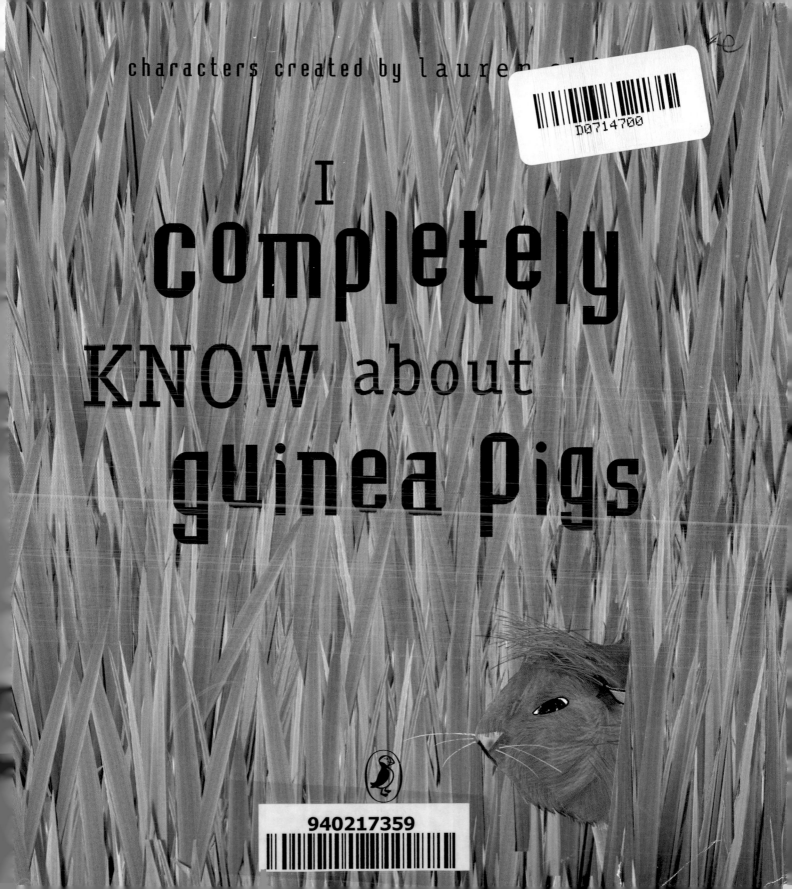

Charlie and Lola ®

Text based on the script written by Paul Larson and Laura Beaumont

Illustrations from the TV animation

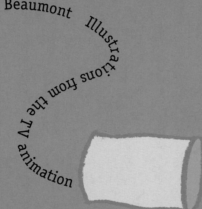

produced by Tiger Aspect

PUFFIN BOOKS
Published by the Penguin Group: London, New York, Australia,
Canada, India, Ireland, New Zealand and South Africa
Penguin Books Ltd, Registered Offices: 80 Strand, London WC2R 0RL, England

puffinbooks.com

First published 2008
Published in this edition 2012
003
Made and printed in China
ISBN: 978-0-141-50232-8

I have this little sister Lola.
She is small and very funny.
At the moment Lola is...
"What ARE you doing at the moment, Lola?"

"I am being a
guinea pig,"
says Lola.

I say, "Why?"

"Because I really like
guinea pigs.
And maybe, if Mrs Hanson
lets me, I can bring Bert, our
class **guinea pig**, home for the
school holidays."

"Have you asked Mum?"

"Yes," says Lola.
"She said it will be

completely

FINE."

The next day at school, Lola says,
"Lotta, do you know ALL about guinea pigs?"
And Lotta says, "There are lots of DIFFERENT
kinds of guinea pig...

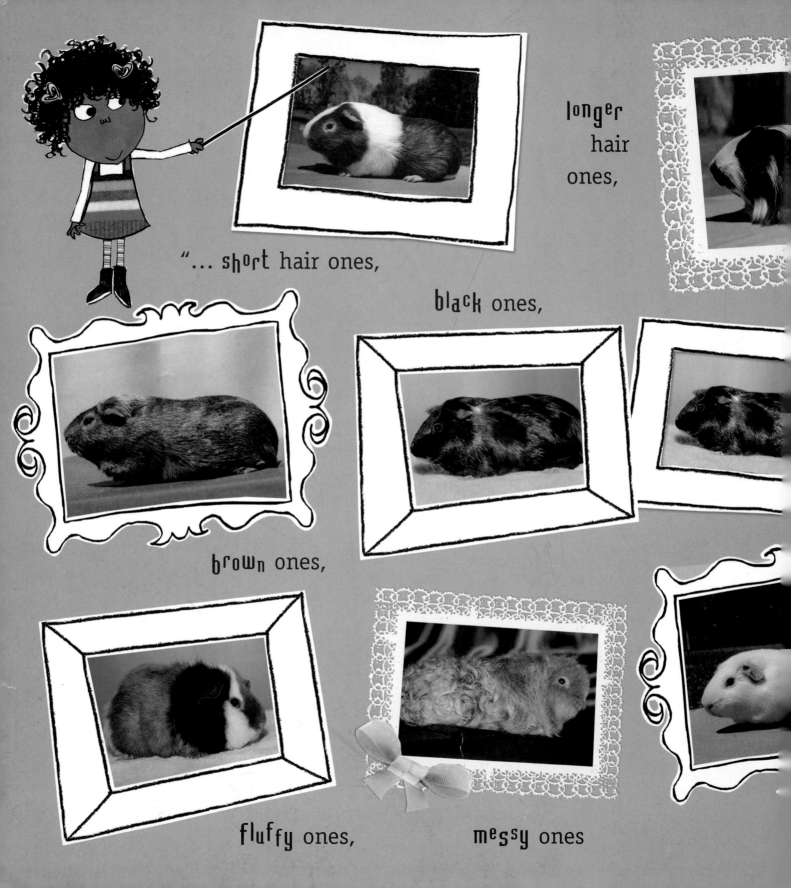

longer hair ones,

"... short hair ones,

black ones,

brown ones,

fluffy ones,

messy ones

brown
and
black
ones,

nd there are
tidy ones."

"I thought Bert was a girl guinea pig,"
says Lola. "He looks
like a girl, because his hair's all pretty."

Mini says, "No, Bert's a boy guinea pig."

"How do you know all
about guinea pigs?" says Lotta.

"Because I've got one at home...
he's called **Fluffy** and he
comes from Peruuuuuu."

"Peruuuu?" say Lola and Lotta.

"Where is Peruuuuu?"

"It's a very long way away, and in PERU there is lots of long grass.

"Hello!"

"Hello!"

Guinea pigs love long grass
because they are shy.

squeak!

"Hello, I'm in Peruuuuuu!"

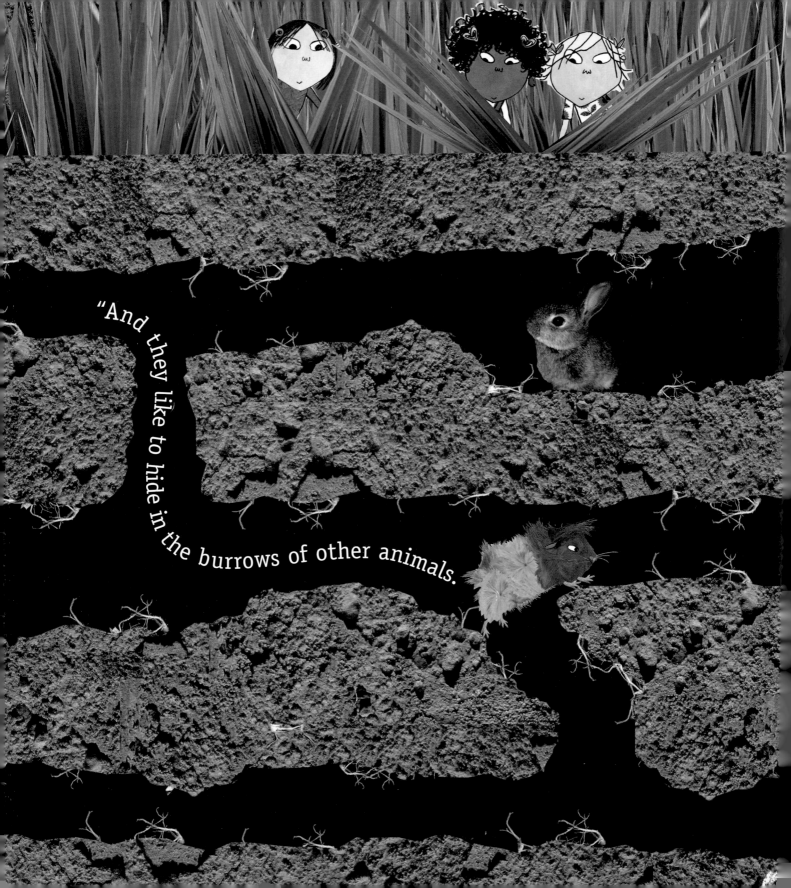

"And they like to hide in the burrows of other animals.

Guinea pigs like to gnaw
on wood and twigs
and things so that
their teeth don't
GROW
really
long.

And they use their whiskers

to see if they can squeeze into...

... different spaces."

Lola says, "I've asked Mrs Hanson if I can take Bert home for the school holidays."

"I've asked Mrs Hanson too," says Bernard. "And I know what they eat!"

"Um... biscuits?"
says Lola.

"No they DON'T, Lola.
Guinea pigs eat
fruit and
vegetables and grass,"
says Mini.

"And
bran,"
says
Bernard.

Lola whispers to Lotta,
"I don't think
Mrs Hanson will choose me
to take Bert home
because **they** know
everything about
guinea pigs and
I don't."

"Oooh, please pick ME,
please
PICK ME,"
says Lola.

And Lola **does** get picked!
So on the way home I say, "Do you know how to look after Bert?"

"Yes I do, Charlie. Mrs Hanson told me **everything** after the class. She said...

I have to give him clean
water every day

and new straw for his bed,

and he mustn't stay outside
at night-time because it
gets **really** cold,

and you must ALWAYS
wash your hands after holding him,

and he likes to eat
fruit and vegetables,

but NOT
potatoes, Charlie.

You must **never**
ever
give a guinea pig
potato...

or crisps."

Then Lola says,
 "And don't you think
Bert looks like a girl?"

 "I don't know," I say.

"Well, I think he looks like
 a girl," says Lola.

 "There!
  A bed for Bert.
There you go, Bert!

If you were my very
 OWN guinea pig,

I would always take you
        shopping with Mum...

and I would
    take you to the
    cinema...

Then I say,
        "Do you want to play
Snap with me, Lola?"

        "No thank you,
Charlie. I am stroking
        Bert because I don't
want him to be lonely."

    "How could he get
lonely! You haven't
        left him for one
    single moment!"

Later I say,
"Dad has made this for your
guinea pig run!"

"Oh goody!" says Lola.
"My guinea pig run is full of **adventures!**

Bert is just going to completely LOVE IT."

"Ready... steady... GO!

Look, Charlie, look at Bert!

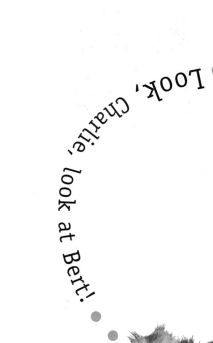

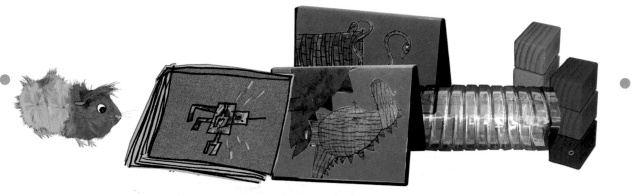

He's going really fast!"

"Bert?

BERT...?

BERT?!

Where is he?

Charlie!

Bert is
completely,
extremely
GONE!"

"Bert?"

"Bert!"

"Maybe he didn't like me," says Lola.
"Maybe he's run away."

And I say, "He hasn't run away.
He has to be here
somewhere."

The next day we STILL

can't find Bert.

"Oh no!
What am I going
to say to Mrs Hanson?"
says Lola.

But then Lola
hears a noise.
"Huh?
Squeaking!"
says Lola.

"It's coming
from over
there..."

And I say, "I don't think Bert is a boy, Lola."
"What do you mean?" says Lola.
"I think Bert has had babies."
And Lola says, "I said he was a girl!"